This Is My Body
and
It Belongs To Me!

This Is My Body
and
It Belongs To Me!

An introduction to the prevention of child sexual abuse for children from 3 years of age and older... and how to respond

Alisha Hawthorne-Martinez, LCSW

ISBN: 978-1-365-31019-5

PublishNation LLC
www.publishnation.net

Printing is made possible by a grant from the Governors Charity Ball and the Rotary del Sol Foundation.

*For my clients who have taught me
the power of hope.*

ACKNOWLEDGEMENTS

I would like to say thank you first and foremost to my God for lighting my way in my career of helping and healing. I'd also like to thank my clients who have taught me so much about the power of hope, healing, and forgiveness; and my family, grandparents, parents, brother, husband, and children who have supported me on each and every journey. I'd like to offer a very special thanks to my grandmother Jerilyn Hawthorne for helping my creativity flow and to Tony Pino for believing in me.

My name is Sara and I am a girl:

A her

A she.

My name is Jason and I am a boy:

A him

A he.

We are both people! In many ways we are the same, but different too!

We both have bodies that are our own! We both have feelings just like you!

I am a girl, and my body belongs to me.

I have girl parts; breasts and a vagina are what I know their names to be.

These are the areas my swimsuit covers and they aren't for anyone else to see;

For this is my body, and it belongs to me!

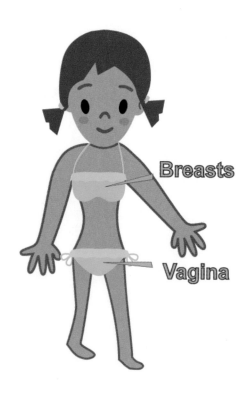

My body is mine, from the top of my head to my little toes.

Only I can say what touch is okay and what touch goes!

I am a boy, and my body belongs to me.

I have boy parts; penis and testicles are what I know their names to be.

These are the areas my swimsuit covers, and they aren't for anyone else to see

For this is my body, and it belongs to me!

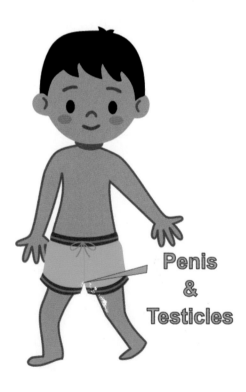

Penis
&
Testicles

My body is mine from the top of my head to my little toes.

Only I can say what touch is okay and what touch goes!

There is safe touch and unsafe touch.

It's important for me to know!

Touch that makes me feel safe and sound,

Like hugs from my parents is the kind of touch I want around!

The touch I don't like, or that makes me feel sad,

Is the kind of touch that I can call bad!

Any touch that's on my swimsuit area is not okay,

Or touch that is uncomfortable in any way!

Unless....

My parent or guardian needs to help clean me,

Or something hurts and my parents need to see!

Or sometimes a doctor needs to check my body, and I have my parents with me!

These are times it is ok for someone else to touch the private areas that belong to me!

One thing I can do with my family

is make up a code word or hand signal just for me!

If ever I feel nervous with someone I am around,

I can just say the code word

Or give a sign to tell without making a sound.

If someone ever wants to touch my private parts,

And I feel weird, or yucky, or scared……

I'll be prepared!

I'll yell "NO, this is my body and it belongs to me not you!"

I'll run to a grown up and ask for help! They'll know what to do!

If someone asks me to touch their private parts,

I'll say "NO!"

Then straight to a safe grown up I will go!

If someone touches me in an unsafe way,

There are some bad things they may say:

Like not to tell,

Or not to yell,

Or that no one will believe what I say,

Or something meant to scare my voice away.

Even though I may feel afraid, I will be brave!

And, now I'll know what to do and what to say!

I won't let anyone take my voice away!

I know that I will be believed by grownups who protect me!

It will take courage, but strong and brave I will be!

I will tell someone I trust about the unsafe touch.

I'll let them know I need their help so much!

When I tell a grown up that someone touched me in an unsafe way

They may not know the words to say.

They may feel very sad or very mad.

But I will remember that unsafe touch is bad!

And they are not mad or sad at me

But at the person who didn't listen that this is MY body.

The grown up I tell may ask for help for me,

From the helpers in my world like doctors, or police, or a counselor to help me see,

That I'm strong, and that I am right! This is my body, and it belongs to me!

So remember, boy or girl, he or she,

This is my body, and it belongs to me!

And your body belongs to you!

And now you know what to do,

To help keep unsafe touch away from you!

And how to ask for help if you need to!

Tips for Parents

1. Safe touch and unsafe touch can be a difficult topic for adults to speak about with their kids. Introducing it at a young age helps ease the process of communication, and assists children in developing protective capacities at an early age.

2. The idea of "good touch/bad touch" has shown to be confusing to children, as all touch was meant to feel good. Safe touch and unsafe touch are terms that are easier for children to grasp.

3. Develop a code word or phrase with your child to communicate with you privately if they are feeling unsafe. This code word or phrase can be anything your child chooses and can remember. If your child uses the code word you should remove him/her from the situation and ask why they were feeling unsafe.

4. Many of the victims that I treat report that they did not disclose the abuse to their parents or guardians

because they did not think they would be believed. Let your children know you believe them.

5. The vast majority of sexual abuse is not perpetrated by a stranger, but by a trusted individual. This often contributes to a child's fear that he or she will not be believed. Show your children that you trust them through communication and support.

6. If your children report sexual abuse tell them you believe them and notify the police and your local Children Youth and Families Department. After making the calls ask your child if there is anything you can do for them. Often times children will have a need that we failed to think of, like the replacement of clothing items or sheets. Sometimes they just ask for comfort. Do not destroy materials that police may need.

7. Frequently check in with children on their safety. After a sleep over, or other event, ask your child, "Did you feel safe?".

8. Remember, sexual abuse is never the victim's fault.

About the Author

Alisha Hawthorne-Martinez is a Licensed Clinical Social Worker. She is the CEO of Second Chance Counseling, LLC in Farmington NM, and the CEO of The Coalition to Prevent Child Sexual Abuse, a New Mexico non-profit organization. Her practice offers home based family centered services, and specializes in treating trauma and youth with problem sexual behaviors. Alisha also does practicum advisement for New Mexico Highlands University and clinical supervision for core service agencies in her area. When she is not working Alisha can be found spending time with her loving husband and children.